Sam Usher

FREE

templar
books

When I woke up
this morning,
one of the birds
was poorly.

I said, "Grandad,
we have to do something!"

So we made him a cosy bed and
Grandad found his book of bird facts.

We gave him a drink of water and Grandad said,
"Look! He's getting better already.
Let's put him back in the garden."

I said, "Oh, do we have to?"

And Grandad said,
"Yes I think so.
He won't want to be
cooped up in here."

So we put him
back outside,
and we thought,
that's that.

It was time for breakfast so we weighed the flour,

poured the milk, cracked the eggs, mixed it up . . .

. . . and flipped the pancakes.

And I said, "Grandad!
Look who it is!"

"Maybe he's hungry.
Can we give him some of our pancakes?"

And Grandad said, "Let's see if he likes
berries instead."

So we put him by
the blackberry bush,
and we thought,
that's that.

When it was time for lunch
we sliced some bread,

found the fillings . . .

. . . and made triple-deckers.

And I said, "Grandad! Look who it is!"

"Do you think he might be lonely?"

And Grandad said, "He might be. Let's take him outside in case any of his friends show up."

So we put him
by the birdbath,
and we thought,
that's that.

At teatime, we chose
our favourite cups,

boiled the kettle,

filled the teapot

and found the biscuits.

And I said, "Grandad!
Look who it is!
I think he likes us,
he keeps coming back."

We spent the rest of the afternoon together.

And I said,
"Grandad, please can he stay forever?"

But Grandad said,
"I think he'll be happier if he's free.
Look, we need to find a tree like this and
help him find his way home."

So we gathered our expedition equipment . . .

. . . and I said, "Look, Grandad, there's the tree,
right at the top of that mountain!"

It was a long
way away . . .

. . . but we made it!

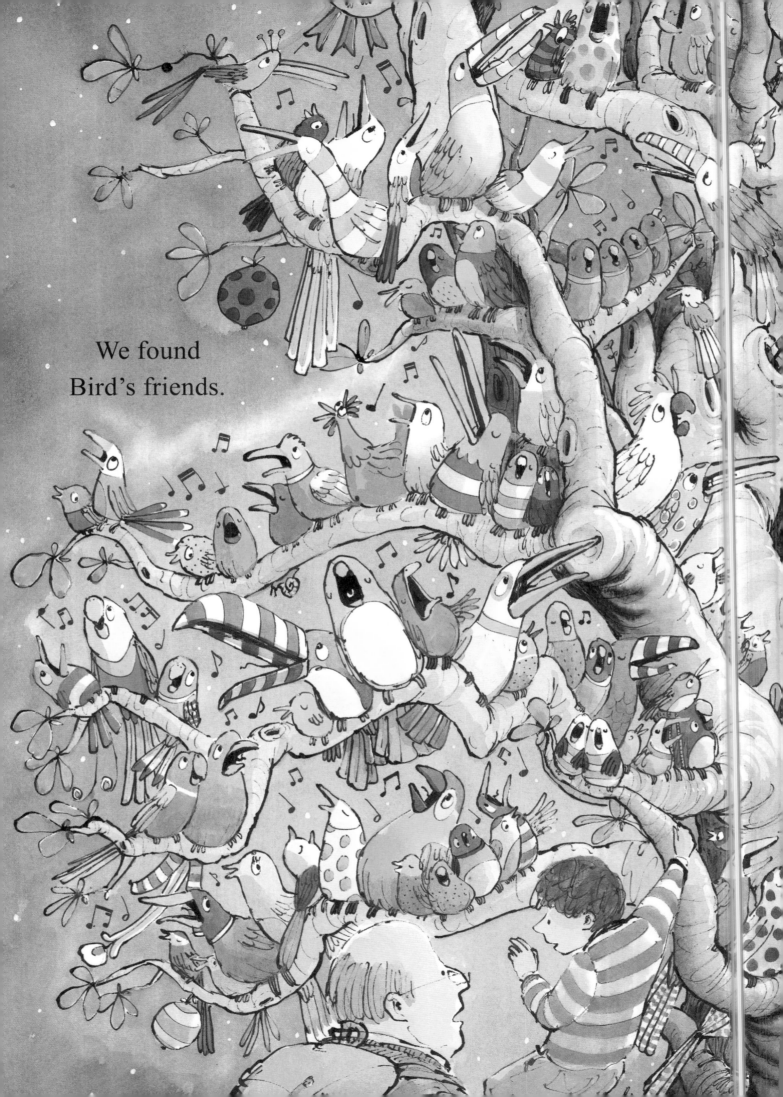

We found
Bird's friends.

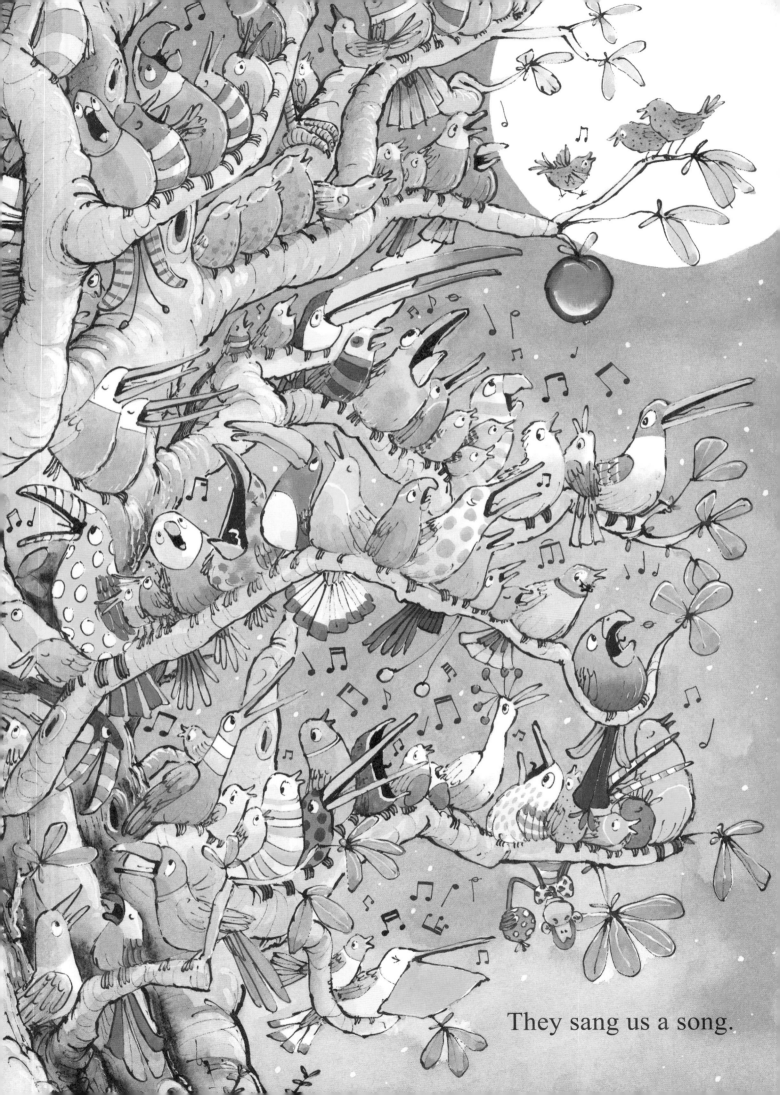

They sang us a song.

And shared their midnight feast.

Then they
flew us all the
way home!

And we were back
in time for breakfast.

Grandad said,
"Our little bird
will be happy now
he's flying free with
all his friends."
And I agreed.

But I hope he visits
again tomorrow.